For Tsuguko, Noriko, and Ayako, and
all the children of the world

Acknowledgments
A word of appreciation to the scientists, researchers, organizations, institutes and project teams
from the Arctic to the Antarctic who, through the Icebridge Forum, generously gave of their time in
contributing information and photographs on ice and ice sheets, polar seas and ocean currents, as well
as the activities, distribution and habits of birds, marine mammals, fish, reptiles and other animals.

Special thanks to: Gary Allport, Eugenio Aramiste, Robert Ballard, Mike Beedell, Ian Boyd,
Fred Bruemmer, Grahame Clarke, Luc Desjardins, Scott Eckert, Whit Fraser, Martin Ghisler, Aleqa
Hammond, Richard Harrington, Patricia Hayward, Rachel Massey, Morton Meldgaard, Carla Penz,
Tove Søvndahl Petersen, Pamela Plotkin, Hugo Rainey, Claudio Rojo Sanchez, William Sladen, Bob Srygley,
David St. Aubin, Henrik Højmark Thomsen, Itaru Uchida, Peter Wadhams, Thomas Webster and Richard
Young and the following organizations and institutes: The Airlie Foundation; BirdLife International; British
Ornithological Society; British Antarctic Survey; Cambridge University, INDI; Canadian Ice Service,
Environment Canada; Canadian Museum of Nature; Canadian Polar Commission; Danish Polar Center;
Geological Survey of Denmark and Greenland; Greenland Home Rule Government; Gulf Coast
Research Laboratory; Mystic Marinelife Aquarium; Sea Research Foundation; Sea World; UNICEF.

and M et M, Co. Ltd.
We wish also to acknowledge the contributions of Lille Huggett,
Group Desgagnés Inc. and the Mathilda Desgagnés.

Kodansha America Inc.
114 Fifth Avenue, New York, New York 10011, U.S.A.
Kodansha International Ltd.
17-14 Otowa 1-chome, Bunkyo-ku, Tokyo 112-8652, Japan
Published in 1998 by Kodansha America, Inc. by arrangement with Kodansha Ltd, Tokyo.

Written by Her Imperial Highness Princess Hisako of Takamado and art by Warabé Aska.
Originally published in 1998 by Kodansha Ltd, Tokyo by arrangement with Icebridge.
The author and the artist have asserted their moral rights to be known as the
author and the artist of the work.

Her Imperial Highness Princess Takamado

Lulie the Iceberg

Art by Warabé Aska

Kodansha International

New York • Tokyo • London

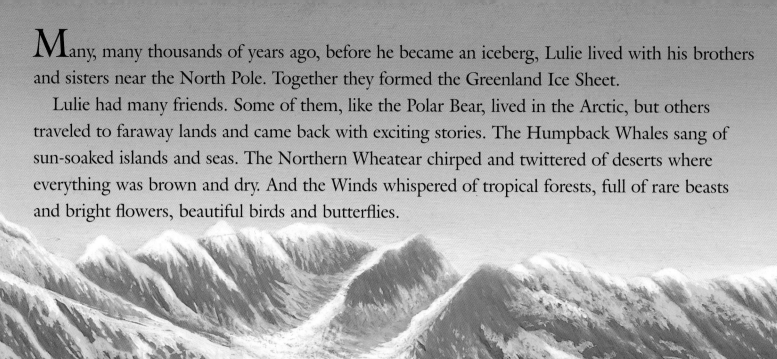

Many, many thousands of years ago, before he became an iceberg, Lulie lived with his brothers and sisters near the North Pole. Together they formed the Greenland Ice Sheet.

Lulie had many friends. Some of them, like the Polar Bear, lived in the Arctic, but others traveled to faraway lands and came back with exciting stories. The Humpback Whales sang of sun-soaked islands and seas. The Northern Wheatear chirped and twittered of deserts where everything was brown and dry. And the Winds whispered of tropical forests, full of rare beasts and bright flowers, beautiful birds and butterflies.

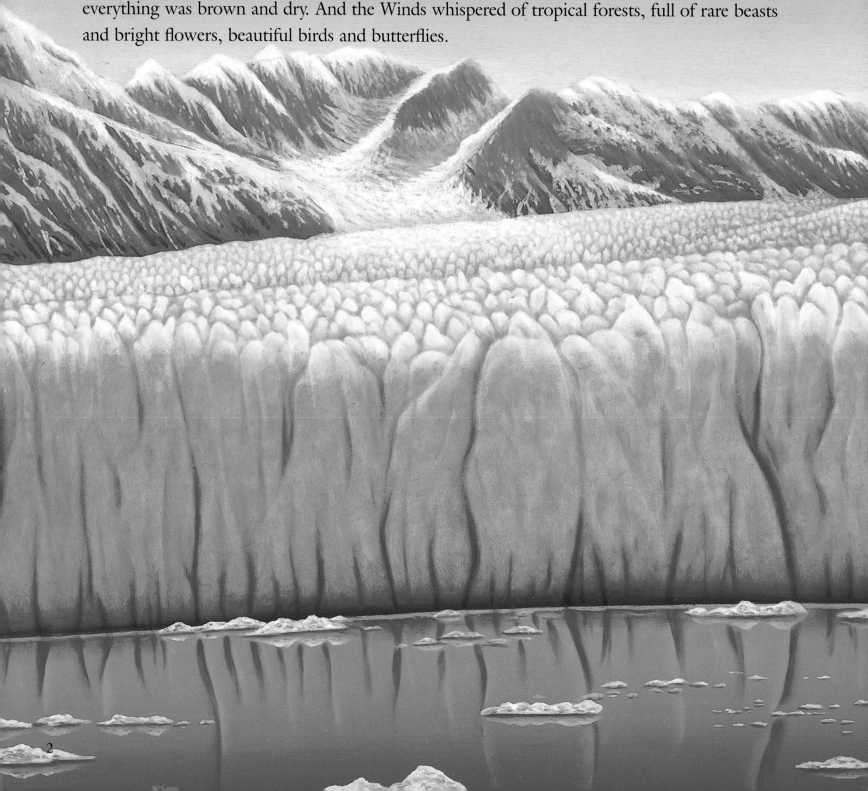

But, above all, Lulie liked to hear Kiki, the Arctic Tern, tell him of the Ice on the Other Side of the Hot Places, and of the Elders who dwelled there. "They are so old!" she said in hushed tones. "And they are so wise! The Winds say that the Elders know all that's happened since the beginning of time."

Lulie tingled with excitement. "One day I'm going to see the Ice on the Other Side and meet the Elders myself!" he said.

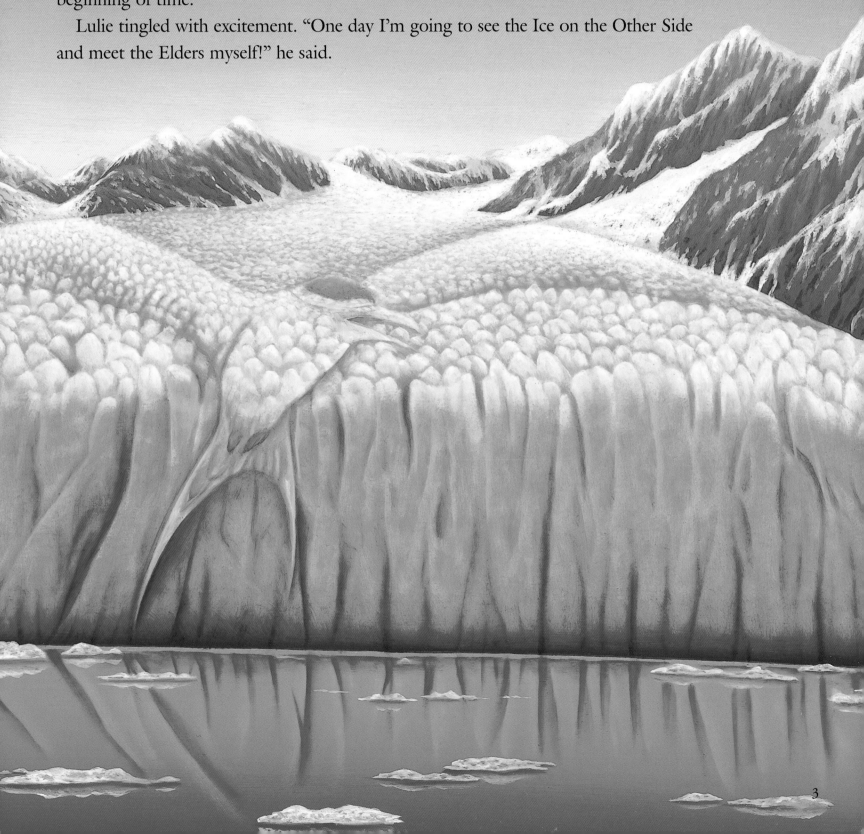

As time passed, Lulie gradually moved from the center of the ice sheet toward the sea. Soon he would become an iceberg. Kiki's tales continued to fascinate Lulie, especially when she spoke of such exciting creatures as the Penguins.

"They're black and white birds that swim like fish and waddle about on the ice," she said.

Lulie longed to see them. "Do you think they'd play on my back?"

In September, after Kiki had headed south, Lulie started to feel the movement in the ice around him.

Then one day, with sharp crackling noises and a deafening roar, Lulie slowly broke off. First the sea swallowed him into its depths, then he rose, faster and faster, till at last he burst through the surface. There followed much popping and crackling of air bubbles. And there he was—Lulie the new Iceberg!

4

His friends gathered around him. "Don't go," said the Polar Bear. "When you get to the Hot Places, you will melt!" But Lulie was determined to go.

"Good luck!" The Bowhead Whale, knowing he would never travel south himself, gave Lulie a nudge and a push to start him off. The Narwhals lifted and crossed their tusks and the Belugas squealed their good-byes.

6

As he drifted past, all his friends cheered him on. The Humpbacks called out, "Soon we will be heading south, too. Good luck!"

So, this was how Lulie began his journey—sad to leave his friends, but excited to be on his way. Lulie drifted with the current down past Canada toward the United States.

The Puffins flew out to greet him. "You must get onto the right current, cross to the other side of the Atlantic, then go south," they said. "If you continue down the coastline here, the Gulf Stream will start pushing you back."

Drifting across would take a long time. *I wonder if I could go faster?* Lulie thought. Just then, some Dolphins leaped and circled around him. "Hello!" they said. "Can we help?" Lulie explained. The Dolphins tried pushing him, but it did not work. The Dolphins ended up with very, very cold noses! They got a rope from some boys in a fishing boat, hooked it around Lulie and tried pulling. "This is much better!" they said.

The clown-faced Puffins were delighted. They perched on Lulie and had a ride before they flew back to the coast.

9

The Dolphins kept up a friendly chatter and took turns pulling, but when they were off the coast of Spain and Portugal, it was time to part. He thanked them and let them eat the fish that were plentiful around him.

Lulie drifted on past Morocco. Some big black and white birds flew out to see him. Lulie was fascinated. "Are you Penguins?" he asked.

"Oh, no," replied the birds, "we are Storks. We heard about you from the Northern Wheatear, and were eager to meet you. You are very beautiful and so blue! But beware, for it will grow very hot as you move south."

It was true. As Lulie drifted along the coast of Africa, he melted more and more each day. He wept, and his tears spread into the sea.

11

The Winds felt sorry for him. "We will take you to the other side of the Atlantic," they said, "and blow you across the equator."

For many days they blew. The waves lashed at Lulie and broke about him. It was all rather exciting! But one day, as he drew near the Brazilian coast, he spotted a boat that was being tossed about by the waves. As he looked on, a little girl on the boat was swept overboard!

"Stop, stop!" Lulie cried out to the Winds. "You must stop!"

After a pause, the Winds spoke softly, "Stop, you say. It was for your dream of thousands of years that we pushed you along. You are still young, Lulie. We who are older have seen much. Your dream was to see more, to understand. If we stop blowing, you will not be able to move. You may melt away. Will you give up your dream to save the child? It is you who must decide."

Lulie sobbed inside. "I'm sorry to be such a nuisance," he said. "But, please stop."

The Winds stopped blowing and the waves calmed down. The boat moved away in search of the child. Lost in his own thoughts, Lulie drifted along. Why was it that he felt so alone? Time passed. How long, he did not know, when, to his surprise, he looked down to find the little girl climbing onto him. She looked very tired and sat still, snuggled up against him.

"Hello. I'm Lulie," he said. "Are you all right?"

"Yes, thank you," she replied. "My name's Marina. I was very frightened, but the turtle helped me."

Lulie looked and saw a large Leatherback Turtle floating beside him. "Marina needed some fresh water so I brought her to you," the turtle explained. Lulie watched Marina drink and felt warm and tender inside. "Her father is a scientist studying sea turtles. The storm took him by surprise," the Leatherback continued. "But you . . . ! What are you doing here?" Lulie explained.

"My goodness!" said the turtle. "You are a brave one!"

The sun was now beginning to set and its rays were no longer so scorching. It was a great relief for Lulie, but he was worried. Without the sun, Marina would get cold sitting on him.

In the distance Lulie saw a spectacular sight—a formation of large birds with velvety red plumage sweeping across the backdrop of a sunset.

"How wonderful!" Lulie exclaimed.

"They are Scarlet Ibises," said a man's voice. It was Marina's father. Marina let out a squeal of delight. She carefully climbed down to her father and jumped into his arms. "Thank you so much for looking after Marina," he said to Lulie.

The old Leatherback watched from a distance, and, looking satisfied, silently swam away.

The time had come to say good-bye. Marina turned to Lulie. "Thank you," she said. When he saw her beaming smile, Lulie wished for one split second that Marina could have stayed snuggled up to him just a little longer.

At night, the moon and the stars would whisper sweet words of encouragement. Lulie smiled up at them. The thought that he might not get to the Ice on the Other Side made him very sad. But somehow, Marina had left him with a sense of warmth and tenderness. And he felt at one with the sea and the sky.

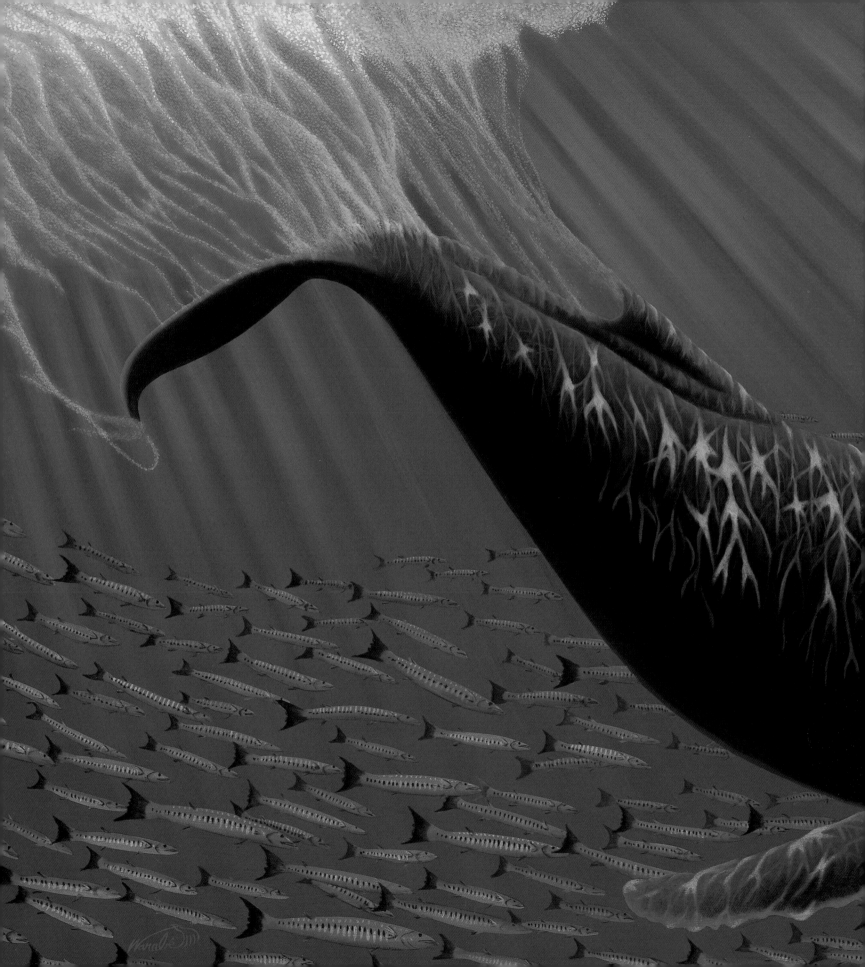

Many days passed. One afternoon, he heard a familiar voice call out "Hello!" He turned to find his friends the Humpback Whales. "Old Mother Leatherback came to tell us you needed our help. We'll give you a shove over the equator and ask the Barracudas to help, too. Once you are across, you must move quickly, for it is a warm current. Hurry, we've no time to lose." Lulie braced himself. The Whales pushed him faster and faster and gave him a final shove. The Barracudas gathered in a huge school. "Thank you-u-u!!" he shouted as he set off. The Winds started to blow from behind. "Our brother winds in the north told us of your willingness to put others before yourself," they whispered gently.

Lulie was blissfully happy. *Everyone is so kind!* he thought. He now
knew that he would never again feel alone. The more he melted,
the bluer he became. Butterflies, who see color very well,
came out to see him, surprised by his beautiful blue.
They fluttered around him to remember his shape
so that they could tell their friends.

Birds, too, flew out to greet him. "Your blue is nearly as blue as mine!" croaked the Blue and Yellow Macaw. The Toco Toucans nodded in agreement. The tropical rainforest was full of exciting new noises and the wind carried to him the sweet scent of strange flowers.

"Hello-o-o!" sang the Southern Humpback Whales as they came to greet him. "Welcome! Our brothers sent us a message that you were on your way."

From the distance came a whitish bird. It somersaulted over Lulie's head and landed on him. It was Kiki! It was nearly four months since he had last seen her. Lulie was a little surprised, for he had never seen her in winter feathers before.

"You've done it, you've done it at last! I knew you would! You should be in Antarctica in no time," Kiki said triumphantly. "I am so proud of you. You are a beautiful iceberg!" Lulie beamed. The ice crystals inside him glowed a gorgeous blue.

Lulie became more and more excited as they made their way down the coasts of Uruguay and Argentina. He wondered how spectacular the Iguacu Falls would be, and thought of the Condors that nest in the high peaks of the Andes. And, again, he felt a warm, tender tingling inside.

Then . . . there it was! The faint but unmistakable smell of ice in the air. Although it was summer, it was cold. Suddenly, in front of him, there appeared ice floes, and in the distance, icebergs. As he neared, he heard them call out, "Welcome! Welcome to Antarctica!" The Winds and the Whales continued to push and push. Finally, there in front of him, the Antarctic continent rose out of the waters in its majestic and awesome splendor.

"How beautiful . . . !" Lulie sighed. Inside him, bubbles burst and exploded with emotion.

It was then that a strange group of black and white creatures darted through the water, charging straight at Lulie. As they approached, they jumped out of the water one after the other and started walking all over him.

Lulie took a deep breath. "Are you . . . are you Penguins?" he asked shyly.

"Yes, yes," they replied, "Emperor Penguins. Welcome to the Antarctic." More penguins clambered on. Lulie tingled and glowed inside with joy.

Lulie soon settled into life in the Antarctic. He adored the many different seals and penguins that crawled and waddled over his back. The Wandering Albatross soared above him and the pretty Snow Petrel flew past. They would all ask him about life in the north. "Tell us about your friends in the Arctic," they would say.

Kiki came and played every day. She was proud of her friend.
He seemed so much wiser now as he told her of his journey.
"I know there were hard moments," he said. "But, I
can only remember the joy of discovering
friendships and the breathtaking
beauty of the planet
we live on."

It was then that Lulie heard the voices. "Welcome," they said. "Welcome . . . "

"It's the Elders . . . !" Lulie tingled with excitement.

The voices vibrated inside him. "In your journey, you heard and felt. You saw. You learned. Now that you can hear our voice, listen and understand. We, the Elders, have dwelled here since the beginning of time. We have always been around you, for we dwell in the land, the air, the seas and in the frozen waters, too. We are the Keepers of the Knowledge and Wisdom of the Earth. And one day, Lulie, you will become one of us."

"Me . . . ! One of the Elders . . . ?"

All the crystals in him, each a little
time capsule of history, shimmered
and shined a brilliant blue.

33

The days sped by. It was soon February. Kiki the Arctic Tern prepared to head north. She felt very important. For she was the messenger, the official carrier of the message, that Lulie the Iceberg was sending to his friends in the north.

If you see Kiki, ask and she will share Lulie's message with you. But you must promise to listen very, very carefully.

GLOSSARY

Note to reader: This glossary will help you understand Lulie's world, from the land to the seas, sky and beyond. We could not mention all of his friends (there are so many!) but encourage you to learn more about them by visiting your local library or aquarium. Also, be sure to look for Lulie's friends hidden in some of the pictures. (There is a list of all of his friends at the back of the book.)

THE EARTH AND SEA

Before we talk about Lulie's animal friends, we should explain a little about our planet Earth, about the winds and currents that dictated Lulie's course of travel, about the two polar regions and, of course, about ice. It may sound difficult at first, but you will be fascinated as you make many new discoveries. This is just the beginning of your own journey to learn more about our wonderful world and its many hidden mysteries.

The **earth** is like a ball with a rock crust on the outside. This ball is surrounded by a huge "bubble" that is hundreds of miles thick. This bubble is called the **atmosphere**. Without the atmosphere no form of life could exist on Earth and there would be no weather, winds, clouds or rain.

The air in the atmosphere is always moving and influences the weather and temperatures around the world. Air moves from the warm regions to the cold; this movement of air is known as **wind**. It carries the surplus heat from the tropics to the polar zones and acts as the earth's air-conditioning system.

The direction of the movement of air and water is interesting. As the earth spins slowly on its axis, it drags the lower layers of the atmosphere with it. The speed of the winds and their direction change in different areas of the earth. **Ocean currents** follow the wind patterns.

In the two **polar regions**, you can see the **aurora** (shown on the inside cover of the book). The light of the sun and moon is reflected off the ice crystals in the lower atmosphere, producing strange and beautiful effects in the polar skies. Sometimes colorful and sometimes pale white or yellow, they appear as arcs and bands, or as immense glowing curtains blowing in a gentle breeze. The oxygen in our atmosphere produces the green color in the aurora. Auroras can be seen on other planets, too, but the green is special to our planet Earth.

Lulie lived in the Greenland Ice Sheet for many thousands of years. **Greenland** is located near the North Pole and is the largest island in the world. As you look at a map or globe, make sure you look for the North and South Poles. Then you can follow Lulie's journey.

POLAR REGIONS

The two **polar regions** in the north and south have the **coldest climates** on Earth. The main reason is that the earth is shaped like a ball. On the equator, in the middle of the ball, the sun shines directly on to the earth. In the polar regions, at the top and bottom of the ball, the sun is never direct and the rays sometimes just skim the surface. Another reason for the cold is that the earth is tilted on its axis. As the earth orbits the sun, the North Pole faces away from the sun and is in complete darkness from September to March, while the South Pole has continuous sun. From March to September, the situation is reversed.

The **Arctic** is in the north. It is a shallow ocean with permanent sea ice floating in the middle. There is no land underneath this ice and the North Pole is located near its center. In the winter this ice grows to be larger than Canada. Surrounding the Arctic Ocean are North America, Greenland, northern Europe and Asia.

The **Antarctic** is in the south. It is a land mass about twice the size of Australia. Whereas the Arctic is a frozen ocean surrounded by land, the Antarctic is a land mass permanently covered by an ice sheet and surrounded by an ocean. In the winter, the sea ice spreads hundreds of miles (kilometers) into the Southern Ocean and the size of Antarctica seems to double.

When the ice breaks up in the summer, the Southern Ocean has the richest life of any ocean in the world. Like all plants, the algae at the bottom of the food chain rely on carbon dioxide, light and mineral nutrients for their growth and the waters around Antarctica have them in abundance. These algae are plant plankton, and during the summer months, the water looks green because of them. Tiny shrimp-like plankton and fish gather to eat these algae and are in turn eaten by larger fish and squid and then such animals as seals, penguins, sea birds and whales.

ICE

So now, let us talk about **ice**. Normally ice is made of frozen water. But **glacier ice** is actually compressed snow. As snow falls on snow, it squashes the fluffy snow beneath it into the firm snow below. This keeps happening until, under the pressure of its own weight, the snow turns to ice. This process has continued for almost 30 million years in Antarctica. When it melts, it will, of course, turn into fresh water, not the salt water of the sea. Because icebergs are glacier ice, Lulie was able to provide Marina with fresh water to drink.

Here are three basic types of glacier ice. First, an **ice sheet**. There are only two ice sheets in the world, Greenland and Antarctica. An ice sheet is a vast dome-shaped mass of ice that is so thick that the shape of the land underneath it cannot be seen. Parts of the Antarctic ice sheet are up to 13,000 feet (4,000 meters) thick! The second is an **ice cap**. This is a mass of ice usually covering a mountain. The surface will show the outline of the shape of the mountain. The third is an **iceberg**. This is a mass of ice that has broken off from a larger mass such as an ice sheet or a glacier. When an iceberg breaks off it is called **calving**.

Since Lulie is an iceberg—and Lulie's name comes from the Greenlandic word that means iceberg, *iluliaq*—let us talk about them a little more. When an iceberg calves, it sounds at first like ice cubes cracking, then becomes a rumbling, roaring sound like thunder. When it crashes into the ocean, it drags a lot of air down with it and the surface of the water caves in like a bowl. As the ice re-emerges, the air that was dragged down is released and shoots up like geysers, making a whistling sound. Together all these sounds are called **ice music**.

Icebergs also sing in pops and crackles as they move along. These are the sounds of compressed air bubbles that have been trapped for thousands and thousands of years being released into the atmosphere as the ice melts.

Icebergs are worn by wind, waves and currents and develop fascinating and beautiful shapes. Sometimes they resemble castles or cathedrals; at other times arches, bridges and even animals. Icebergs with a lot of air inside them float high and are more white. The older ice-bergs with more compressed air are bluer. Only the "tip of the iceberg" shows above water, with perhaps four-fifths being below the surface. That's why ships need to be cautious. Some icebergs are as big as small countries, many are the size of football fields and others are as tall as famous monuments!

Some icebergs travel tremendous distances. There have been reported iceberg sightings down the Canadian coast, across to the Azores and North Africa. There are also records of an Arctic iceberg that reached Bermuda and an Antarctic iceberg that nearly made it to Rio de Janeiro!

While glaciers are fresh water, **sea ice** is frozen sea water. The ice floes that Lulie saw first when he arrived in the Antarctic were sea ice.

Finally, one last word about learning from ice. It used to be said in Greenland and the Canadian Arctic that the ice contained all the traditions of the people because it was there before them and existed throughout their history. Each person was taught to respect the ice so that he could learn from it.

Today, scientists recognize the knowledge and history that dwells in the ice sheets. Scientists from many different countries are conducting research in the polar regions. One example is the study of **ice cores.** By drilling into the ice sheets with a hollow, tube-shaped drill, they extract long thin pieces of ice. These ice cores are a record of the earth's history, for they are made up of the snow that fell thousands, perhaps millions of years ago. When scientists study such things as the tiny bubbles of gas, particles of dust and pollen and fragments of insects in the ice cores, they are able to learn about the changes in the world's atmosphere, climate and wildlife and how to protect it in the future.

LULIE'S FRIENDS OF THE LAND, SEA AND AIR

Now, let us look at some of Lulie's friends in detail. In order to make it easier to understand where it is that his friends live, we have divided them into those that live all year in the Arctic, those that live all year in the Antarctic and those that winter, or actually live, in the regions in between. Because Lulie's special friend, Kiki the Arctic Tern, lives in all three areas, we will start off this section with the **Arctic Tern**.

Arctic Tern

Arctic Terns are amazing birds. They breed in the northern hemisphere and polar regions, then they fly south to winter on the edge of the Antarctic. Many of them travel the same route as Lulie. Their round-trip flight is almost the same distance as the circumference of the globe!

All terns have distinctly long, narrow wings, pointed bills and, usually, forked tails. Compared to other terns, Arctic Terns have short legs and very long wings. They are excellent fliers and are able to cope with blustery winds. Kiki's name comes from the call of the tern, which is quite clear and high and sounds like "keer-keer."

As with many other birds, the tern's summer plumage is more dramatic because that is when they breed. The distinctive black cap and coral-red bill and legs are summer colors. In winter, the black cap becomes a narrow band and the bill and legs turn a reddish black. They look a little like the Lone Ranger. Lulie knows Kiki only in her summer plumage and is surprised to see her looking different in the Antarctic.

LULIE'S FRIENDS IN THE ARCTIC

Arctic Whales

Of all the whale and dolphin species in the world, these **Arctic Whales** are the only ones to spend their entire lives around ice.

The **Bowhead Whales** are the largest of the three. They can reach 60 feet (18 meters) long and weigh up to 110 tons (100 tonnes). The head takes up one-third of the body and the mouth has 600 baleen plates that hang from the upper jaw like vertical blinds. The Bowheads have no teeth but use this baleen to filter the krill (tiny shrimplike plankton) that is their main diet. Nine other species of whale have baleen, but none is as long or as dense as those of the Bowheads.

The **Narwhals** are strange-looking creatures with an upper left tooth that grows into a spiral tusk of up to 9 feet (3 meters). The tooth pierces through their upper lip and always spirals counterclockwise. The whales themselves are about 15 feet (4.5 meters) long. The females do not usually have a tusk. It is thought that the Narwhal gave rise to the myth of the unicorn.

The **Belugas** are white whales. Their chatter and singing earned them the name "sea canary." The Belugas have teeth, but swallow whole the fish, squid and other food that they capture by sucking in. Before they swallow, however, they squeeze out the salt sea water with their tongue. The Belugas are highly social and love to play and chatter.

Polar Bear

Of the eight bear species in the world, Polar Bears and Grizzly or Brown Bears are the largest. The two bears look and act differently, but they are closely related. In fact, Polar Bears evolved from the Brown Bears during the last Ice Age.

Polar Bears are meat-eating predators, and are extremely well adapted to living in the Arctic environment. Good insulation is ensured by a double-layered coat of hollow outer guard hairs and a thick undercoat, by a skin that is black so that it absorbs heat and by a thick layer of fat to prevent loss of body heat. The soles of its feet are well covered with fur to prevent frostbite and the foot pads have thousands of tiny bumps to stop the bear from slipping and sliding on the ice. Their feet are partially webbed and the bears are superb swimmers and divers.

Walrus

The Walrus is probably the most recognizable of the three seals to appear in *Lulie*. Its distinguishing features are the huge tusks that grow up to 3 feet (1 meter) long and the ample moustache consisting of about 500 coarse, but sensitive, whiskers. Another characteristic is the extremely thick skin that falls in creases and folds.

LULIE'S FRIENDS IN THE ANTARCTIC

Penguins

All penguins live in the southern hemisphere (except for the Galapagos Penguin). Penguins have bodies that are adapted to the cold. The tightly overlapping feathers are small and hard and cover every square millimeter of the body. The base of each feather is fluffy and traps the air warmed by the body like thermal underwear. If they get hot, penguins fluff up their feathers and hold their flippers out from their bodies to release the trapped warm air. When you see them on their stomachs with their feet stretched backwards, they are releasing the heat through the soles of their feet.

Penguins have adapted themselves for a life in the water with bodies that are compact and streamlined. They virtually fly underwater, using their stiff, strong flippers like wings to propel them forward in the sea.

The largest of the penguins, the **Emperor,** is 42 inches (115 cm) tall and weighs nearly 90 pounds (40 kg). Emperors form colonies of many thousands. No other bird is better adapted to the bitter cold. Each season the male Emperor places .the newly laid egg on his feet and tucks it into his brood pouch to keep warm while the female leaves to find food at sea. When she returns two months later the chick has hatched and ready to meet its mother.

Weddell Seal

Weddell Seals are large and bulky with small heads. They seem to smile at you but have splendidly strong teeth that they use to keep breathing holes open in the ice during winter. Their bodies are specially adapted to deep diving. Seals empty their lungs of air to keep themselves from floating and store the oxygen they need in their blood and muscles. They can frequently dive to depths of 1,000 to 1,300 feet (300 to 400 meters). They also make shallow dives where they stay submerged for over 70 minutes.

LULIE'S FRIENDS IN BETWEEN

Humpback Whale

The Humpbacks are large baleen whales that are about 45 feet (15 meters) long and that weigh about 40 tons (41 tonnes). They are very active and acrobatic, often breaching (leaping out of the water) or lying on their sides smacking the surface of the water with their tails or their long, wing-like fins. Their name comes from the way they "hump" their back when breaching.

Lulie's friends, the Humpbacks from the north, did not go with him across the equator. The whales in the north and south are the same species, but separate groups. They spend their respective summers in the Arctic or Antarctic because the cold seas provide abundant food then. But they do not normally cross the equator, nor do they meet.

How can scientists distinguish one Humpback from another? Humpbacks raise their tail flukes high into the air before making a deep dive. Each tail has a black and white pattern on it which is particular to that whale. They act like fingerprints do for people.

Many animals "sing," but the song of the male Humpbacks is considered to be the longest and most complex of all.

Dolphins

The dolphins that see Lulie off when he leaves the Arctic are **Atlantic Whitesided Dolphins**. They are fast swimmers and very acrobatic. They live only in the cooler waters of the north Atlantic.

The dolphins that help Lulie cross from the coast of North America to the Iberian Peninsula are the **Common Dolphins**. They can be found in nearly all of the world's temperate and tropical seas, and may travel in groups of several hundred, even several thousand. They average about 6 feet (2 meters) in length and have a distinctive hourglass pattern and a well-defined beak.

Many dolphins are very active and very vocal. They will play in the pressure wave created by whales and will often follow ships and play in the wake.

Orca

Orcas are toothed whales and are also called Killer Whales. They eat most marine creatures, from dolphins to herrings. Apart from the glossy black and white markings, the most distinctive feature of the Orcas is the 5 foot (1.5 meter) tall dorsal (back) fin of the male.

Orcas live in family groups called **pods** with as many as 25 or 30 others and have strong social bonds. Each pod has its own "dialect" in the sounds and calls it uses. They hunt together in pods, sharing the food, much like lions or wolves may do on land. On average, Orca males live to be about 30 years old and females about 50.

Atlantic Puffin

Atlantic Puffins belong to the Auk family. They are popular for their clownlike faces and curious waddling walk. The distinguishing feature is the large, flat, triangular bill, in a bright shade of red, yellow and blue. In winter they have a smaller, less colorful bill. They are chunky birds and look stubby even when flying. They breed in holes in the turf or among the rocks of the sea islands.

White Stork

White Storks have lived close to people for several centuries and use chimneys, roof towers and haystacks as their nesting sites when they return from their wintering grounds in spring. It must be the association of the season and chimneys that gave them their legendary role in the arrival of babies. Storks fly only during the morning and early afternoon.

Leatherback Turtle

The Leatherback Turtles are the largest of the of the eight sea turtle species in the world. They weigh an average of 800 pounds (360 kg) and are about 64 inches (160 cm) long. Sea turtles have lived on this planet for over 150 million years (man goes back only 6 million)! All sea turtles live in saltwater and drink it, excreting the excess salt through the tear ducts. They have no teeth, but strong jaws, and though they have good eyesight underwater and can see color, on land their vision is poor.

Female Leatherbacks lay their eggs on a sandy beach in a very deep nest cavity. They spend more time and effort than any other species in disguising the exact location of the egg chamber. Nest concealment sometimes takes more than 30 minutes. Tiring work for such heavy marine creatures!

Leatherback Turtles dive the deepest and travel the farthest of any sea turtle. They dive to depths of 3,300 feet (1,000 meters) and are able to stay submerged and active for over 25 minutes. They are also known to frequent cold waters. It was lucky for Marina that it was a Leatherback that took her to Lulie, for other turtles may have found the waters around him too cold!

Scarlet Ibis

The Scarlet Ibis is a spectacular flame-red bird that lives in the wetlands and mangrove swamps of South America. When they are in their nests, the trees look like they are covered with brilliant red blossoms.

Surprisingly, the Scarlet Ibis chicks are covered in black down. When the birds are in their third year, they are ready to breed. That is when their red plumage appears, leaving only the tips of their wings black. The legs are completely red and even the bill is tinged red.

Great Barracuda

Barracudas have lean, elongated, metallic-colored bodies and very large teeth. Barracudas as young fish often come together in large schools and are very curious about unusual objects such as divers, boats and, possibly, icebergs! They are very fast and can reach speeds of up to 30 mph (50 kph), thereby creating a movement in the water like an advance wave in front of them. Very useful when pushing Lulie.

Toco Toucan, Blue and Yellow Macaw

The tropical rainforest is home to a great number of spectacular creatures.

There are 42 species of toucan in Central and South America; the **Toco Toucans** are one of the largest. Their huge, brightly-colored bills are almost as long as their bodies but are surprisingly light. Their diet is mainly fruit.

The **Macaws** belong to the parrot family (332 species). Their hooked bill is very powerful and is adapted for opening hard nuts, biting chunks out of fruit and grinding seeds into meal. Their legs are thick and strong, with two stout toes facing forward and two backward. Parrots are very vocal and raucous.

LULIE'S JOURNEY

Why not look up on a map which winds and currents helped Lulie reach Antarctica.

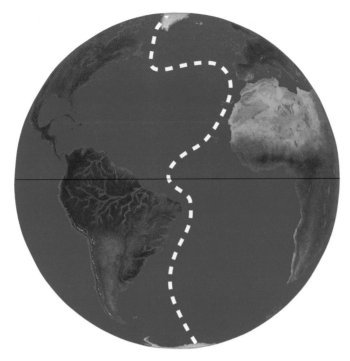

See if you can find Lulie's friends on each page

Pages 2–3: *Hidden*–Arctic Tern

Pages 4–5: Arctic Tern, Beluga, Bowhead Whale, Narwhal, Orca, Polar Bear, Ringed Seal, Walrus; *Hidden*–Arctic Fox, Arctic Hare, Arctic Wolf, Caribou, Humpback Whale, Musk Ox, Snowy Owl

Pages 6–7: Atlantic White-Sided Dolphin, Beluga, Bowhead Whale, Humpback Whale, Great Northern Diver (Common Loon), Gyrfalcon, Thick-Billed Murre, Narwhal, Orca, Polar Bear, Ringed Seal, Walrus, White-Tailed Eagle; *Hidden*–Arctic Fox, Arctic Hare, Arctic Wolf, Caribou, Musk Ox

Pages 8–9: Common Dolphin, Atlantic Puffin

Pages 10–11: White Stork

Pages 14–15: Leatherback Turtle

Pages 16–17: Leatherback Turtle, Scarlet Ibis

Pages 18–19: *Hidden*–Arctic Tern, Beluga, Bowhead Whale, Common Dolphin, Gyrfalcon, Narwhal, Polar Bear

Pages 20–21: Great Barracuda, Humpback Whale

Pages 22–23: Amazonian Yellow-Rumped Cacique, Amydon Butterfly, Barred Leaf Frog, Blue and Yellow Macaw, Green Anole Lizard, Green Iguana, Narcissus Butterfly, Scarlet Macaw, Squirrel Monkey, Toco Toucan

Pages 24–25: Arctic Tern, Humpback Whale

Pages 26–27: Andean Condor

Pages 28–29: Emperor Penguin

Pages 30–31: Arctic Tern, Emperor Penguin, Snow Petrel, Wandering Albatross, Weddell Seal; *Hidden*–Emperor Penguin

Pages 32–33: Arctic Tern

Pages 34–35: Arctic Tern, Emperor Penguin

Cover: Arctic Tern, Humpback Whale

Title page: Arctic Tern, Bowhead Whale

Back cover: Arctic Tern